D0644626

Off-Key

Don't miss Catalina's other magical adventures!

Catalina Incognito
The New Friend Fix
Skateboard Star

BY JENNIFER TORRES

CATALINA INCOGNITO

Off-Key

ILLUSTRATED BY
GLADYS JOSE

ALADDIN
New York London Toronto Sydney New Delhi

ALADDIN

An imprint of Simon & Schuster Children's Publishing Division

1230 Avenue of the Americas, New York, New York 10020

First Aladdin paperback edition July 2022

Text copyright © 2022 by Jennifer Torres

Illustrations copyright © 2022 by Gladys Jose

Also available in an Aladdin hardcover edition.

All rights reserved, including the right of reproduction in whole or in part in any form.

ALADDIN and related logo are registered trademarks of Simon & Schuster, Inc.

For information about special discounts for bulk purchases, please contact Simon & Schuster Special Sales at 1-866-506-1949 or business@simonandschuster.com.

The Simon & Schuster Speakers Bureau can bring authors to your live event. For more information or to book an event contact the Simon & Schuster Speakers Bureau at 1-866-248-3049 or visit our website at www.simonspeakers.com.

Designed by Laura Lyn DiSiena

The illustrations for this book were rendered digitally.

The text of this book was set in Century Schoolbook.

Manufactured in the United States of America 0622 OFF

2 4 6 8 10 9 7 5 3 1

Library of Congress Control Number 2021945046

ISBN 9781534483101 (hc)

ISBN 9781534483095 (pbk)

ISBN 9781534483118 (ebook)

For Amanda

Contents

CHAPTER 1

FLUTTER

It's after school on Monday, and the auditorium is filled with students practicing for the Valle Grande Elementary talent show. Auditions are at the end of this week.

I creep past a group of fourth graders tap-dancing side by side next to a second grader performing a tae kwon do demonstration.

Behind them, Aaron Chu, a third grader in my class, rehearses his magic act. He swooshes his cape.

He waves his hands over a black top hat. He taps the edge of the hat with his wand. I watch, waiting to see what will happen.

When nothing does, Aaron peers into the hat and shrugs.

I shudder. I'd hate for *my* act to go wrong. That's why I'm sneaking through the auditorium. Somewhere in this room is the formula for a perfect performance, and I'm going to find it. I need to make sure my group has an amazing audition and gets picked for the show.

The best part is, none of the other kids notice me. Not really. When they look in my direction, all they see is a yellow-winged butterfly. That's because last summer my tía abuela—her name is Catalina Castañeda too—gave me a special sewing kit.

It might not *look* very special, just an old, worn-out velvet pouch. But the needle and thread inside have the power to sew magical disguises.

Over the weekend, I sewed butterfly wings onto one of my old sweaters. (It was missing a button anyway. I could have sewn on a new one, but it wouldn't have matched the others, and I can't stand it when things don't match.) Then I added antennae to one of my hairbands. The perfect disfraz! Now anyone who sees me thinks I'm a butterfly. I am *incognito*.

Tía Abuela told me to save the magic for times when I *really* need it. Once my spool of silvery magical thread is gone, it's gone for good.

This is one of those times when I need my magic. After all, my bandmates and I will be performing a song that Tía Abuela made famous back when she was still a telenovela actress. We can't make any mistakes.

I flutter behind Esme Galindo and her cousin

Jazmín. They wear swirling blue skirts as they practice a folklórico dance.

Suddenly Jazmín stops in the middle of a step.

"What happened?" Esme asks. "Did you forget what comes next?"

They definitely need more practice.

Jazmín shakes her head. "No, but I thought I saw Catalina."

Uh-oh. Maybe my disfraz isn't working. I duck behind a cardboard tree some fifth graders are using as a prop in their skit.

"Shouldn't she be with her own group?" Esme asks.

"You know Catalina," Jazmín continues. "She probably wanted to give us some of her helpful hints."

Esme giggles, and they start dancing again.

I *might* have a reputation for being a bit of a perfectionist. *Who doesn't want to be perfect?* I almost wonder aloud. Instead I look over my shoulder to make sure the butterfly wings are still attached.

Tía Abuela warned me that the magic would only be as strong as my stitches. And these are coming loose! I need to get out of this disfraz before anyone else notices!

While the fifth graders argue over their lines,

I yank off the wings and slip out of the sweater. I
tuck everything under my arm, then step out from
behind the carboard tree and find my group at the
other side of the auditorium.

We call ourselves Banda La Chispa in honor of
Tía Abuela. Her fans know her as La Chispa, "the
spark," because she was always so bright and daz-
zling onscreen.

Ruthie Rosario sits behind her drum set. Soledad Beltrán has her guitar strapped over her shoulder. Pablo Blanco, my best friend—and biggest rival— stands next to his keyboard, tapping his foot. He scowls when he sees me. "You're late," he says.

Impossible. No one cares about punctuality as much as I do. Except for Pablo, that is. I look down at my watch and frown. Unfortunately, he's right.

"Only thirty-six seconds," I say.

"Thirty-seven," Pablo argues. "And anyway, late is late. Where were you?"

I hesitate. So far I haven't revealed the secret of the magic sewing kit to anyone.

Luckily, Ruthie interrupts before I have to answer.

"Cool hairband!" she says. "Animal accessories are my favorite!"

I feel the top of my head. I'm still wearing the butterfly antennae. "Um, thanks," I mumble, my cheeks going all warm. Pablo snorts. Normally I am perfectly put together.

Soledad hands me the tambourine we borrowed from the music room. "Now that we're all here," she says, "let's run through the song from the very beginning."

Ruthie taps out the rhythm with her drumsticks.

"Uno, dos, tres, cuatro!" Soledad counts. She begins to strum, then nods at Pablo, who presses down on the keys. I start shaking the tambourine. When we get to the chorus, I open my mouth to sing. Only, I can hardly keep up with Ruthie's beat.

Pablo's notes clash with Soledad's chords, and we all sound a little . . . off-key.

When the song ends, I cringe. Part of me wants to run back to that cardboard tree to hide again. Maybe we can still back out of the auditions. Then I remind myself of something Tía Abuela taught me when I was first learning to sew: progress takes practice. *And* patience. Sometimes a *lot* of patience.

"Don't worry," I reassure everyone. "We still have a few more days to get better."

"Are you kidding?" Soledad shouts. "That was amazing! And so much fun! We are obviously going to make the talent show."

But I'm not so sure.

CHAPTER 2

SPECIAL DELIVERY

I can't open the door at first when I get home from school. Something is blocking it. My older sister, Coco, probably dumped her enormous backpack in the entryway. *Again.* This is exactly why I asked Mami to install those special hooks on our bedroom wall. I thought that if the backpacks had a special place to hang, maybe Coco would stop leaving hers on the floor. It doesn't seem to be working.

"Co—" I start to complain as I shove the door

open. Then I look down. It isn't Coco's backpack that's blocking the way. It's a big box. Addressed to me! The postage on top says it came from Colombia.

And the handwriting tells me who sent it: Tía Abuela.

Ever since she retired from acting, Tía Abuela spends most of her time traveling the world. Wherever she goes, she finds a way to send packages home to Valle Grande. Last time, it was stickers for Coco's skateboard. And the time before that, a hand-carved rattle for Baby Carlos, our little brother. This time, it's something for me.

I push the box into the living room, where Papi and Coco are putting on a puppet show for Carlos. Maybe they should audition for the talent show too.

"It's about time you got home," Coco says.

"We almost couldn't resist opening that box," Papi agrees.

Carlos claps his hands, all sticky with the apple-sauce he's been snacking on. I wrinkle my nose and make a mental note not to let him touch whatever's inside the package.

"Well, what are you waiting for?" Coco asks, leaping up from the carpet and flinging the dinosaur puppets off her hands. "Open it!"

Of course I'm going to open it. But first I need the proper tools. Calmly I carry my backpack to the coffee table and set it down. I unzip the middle pouch and take out my school scissors.

Coco groans.

Then I carefully snip the tape along one side of the box. I am about to move on to the next piece of tape when Coco nudges me aside.

"This is going to take forever!" she complains. She kneels beside the box and rips off the rest of the tape with one sharp tug. "There. It's open."

I want to tell Coco that patience makes perfect, but I am just as excited as she is to see what Tía Abuela sent. I lift open the cardboard flaps. The gift is wrapped in tissue paper, with a note card sitting on top.

I take the note card out of the box and read aloud. *"Mi amiga Josefina tells me you are making excellent progress with your sewing. Keep practicing! Sewing can be like magic. But remember what I've told you. The magic is only as strong as your stitches."*

I can imagine Tía Abuela winking behind her cat-eye sunglasses when she wrote those lines. I glance up to see if Papi or Coco suspect that Tía Abuela was writing about *real* magic. They don't, so I keep reading. *"I wanted you to have some new material for your next projects. This fabric is from the fashion shows in Medellín. I can't wait to see what you create with it!"*

I set the note card down and reach into the box. Underneath the tissue paper are bundles of fabric. One piece is icy blue and speckled with silver stars. The largest piece is purple and satiny smooth. There's a zebra print—one of Tía Abuela's favorite patterns—and a piece that shimmers with pink and gold sequins.

Papi takes a velvety green square and uses it to play peekaboo with Carlos. I'm so dazzled by all the fabric that I don't even mind him touching it. *Much.*

"She didn't say anything else?" Papi asks after his next *Boo!* "Nothing about where she's traveling next?"

"I don't think so," I answer. She hardly ever does. Sometimes we try to guess where her next post-card will come from, but it's always a surprise. Papi should know that.

Then Coco picks up the note card. "She did! There's more writing on the back!"

I yank the note from her hand. Coco is right. I can't believe I missed it. Most of the time, I have excellent attention to detail. It's why Tía Abuela trusted me with the magic sewing kit in the first place. I read on. *"Maybe you can show me what you're working on when I come to visit. Your papi* told me you'll be singing in the school talent show. I wouldn't miss it! You know the old saying: 'Quien canta sus males espanta.' 'Whoever sings frightens their worries away.'"

"Is this true?" I ask when I get to the end.

Papi tilts his head and thinks for a moment. "Well, singing *does* put me in a good mood," he says. "So I suppose it's true."

"I'm not asking if the *saying* is true!" I reply. "I mean what Tía Abuela wrote before that. Is it true she's coming to visit?"

Papi laughs. "Surprise!" he says. "I knew Tía Abuela would love to hear you sing. Especially since you'll be performing one of her songs."

Coco takes the zebra-print fabric and whips it around her neck like a cape. "I can finally show her my kick flip!" she exclaims. "And Tía Abuela promised to bring back pictures of the big skate parks in South America."

Even Carlos starts to clap again.

Not me. I sit there, staring at the note.

"What's the matter, Kitty-Cat?" Papi asks. "Aren't you excited to see Tía Abuela?"

I can tell him at least one thing that's the matter: he won't stop calling me "Kitty-Cat." As I've told my family about a zillion times, I'm getting too old for all this kitten stuff.

But that's not *really* what's bothering me. *Of course* I'm excited to see Tía Abuela. I'm especially excited to show her how far my sewing has come. When she started to teach me over the summer, I could barely thread a needle.

But this news has made me even *more* nervous about the talent show audition. What if Banda La Chispa doesn't get picked for the show, and Tía

Abuela travels all this way for nothing?

Or worse, what if we *do* get to perform, and we're terrible?

"I'm excited," I tell Papi finally. "But the band has a lot of practicing to do. *And* I need to get to Stitch and Share."

CHAPTER 3

FOLLOWING INSTRUCTIONS

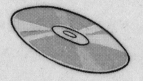

When she gave me the magic sewing kit, Tía Abuela made me promise to go to the Stitch and Share sessions that her best friend, Josefina the Librarian, holds once a week at the Valle Grande Central Library. If I'm going to be responsible for such powerful magic, Tía Abuela wants to make sure I learn how to use it.

As usual, I am the first to arrive. Most of the time, Josefina arranges metal folding chairs in a circle in the library's community room. One by one, we sewists—that's what Josefina calls us—choose a seat and take out our latest project. We share what we're working on, and there's always someone to give advice if we get stuck.

But today I notice something different: a table at the center of the room with a piece of fabric spread over it. Josefina smooths out the wrinkles, then arranges pieces of thin crinkly paper on top. They look a little like puzzle pieces. I am excellent at putting puzzles together. Figuring out exactly where things belong is one of my specialties. Maybe this time *I* can help Josefina for a change.

"What are you working on?" I ask.

"Catalina!" she greets me. "Early as usual. I'm tracing a pattern for a dress I want to sew. Come watch."

I step closer to the table and study the pieces.

"It doesn't *look* very much like a dress," I say before I can stop myself. I slap a hand over my mouth, hoping I haven't made Josefina feel bad.

She laughs and picks up one of the pieces. "Not yet," she agrees. "But soon this will be a sleeve."

She takes the paper and gently drapes it around my arm.

"See?" she asks.

I look down at the pattern piece on my arm and then at the rest of the pieces. I close my eyes and picture them stitched together instead of flat on the table. The dress comes together in my imagination.

"I see it!" I say.

Josefina smiles and places the sleeve pattern back on the fabric. She shows me how to carefully trace around its edge with a chalk pencil to create a sleeve-shaped piece of cloth. She even lets me cut out the piece that will become the dress's skirt. I love following directions step-by-step and making my cutting line smooth and straight.

This might be my favorite Stitch and Share session yet!

But then, as the other sewists begin to arrive and choose their seats, Josefina does something that makes me gasp. The skirt should have been the last pattern piece, but Josefina isn't finished. She uses the chalk pencil to draw a teardrop shape on the fabric and cuts that out too.

"That's not supposed to be there!" I protest. You don't get to add your own pieces to a puzzle. They would have no place to fit. A dress shouldn't be any different from a puzzle. "Isn't that breaking the rules?"

Josefina chuckles again. "Don't worry, Catalina," she says. "I add pockets to all my dresses. That way I can always carry kitty treats with me." She pats the side pocket of the pants she's wearing. "You never know when the library might have another feline visitor."

I gulp. One of the cats that Josefina found wandering in the library was really *me* wearing a magical disfraz.

Luckily, Josefina doesn't seem to suspect anything. She goes on. "Do you know what my favorite part of sewing is?"

"Obviously it's not paying attention to the instructions," I mumble.

"No," Josefina replies. "It's getting the chance to give whatever I create my own personal touch."

Ms. Yoo holds up the jacket she's sewing. "Same here," she says. "This pattern called for a zipper. But I decided to replace it. I wanted to show off some of the antique buttons in my collection."

Mr. Hart nods. "Every time I make a new shirt, I have to widen the collar so that it doesn't feel so tight around my neck."

Tía Abuela gave me the sewing kit because of my careful attention to detail. Because I always follow directions. Now the sewists are telling me they *ignore* the instructions. *On purpose?*

I don't realize my shoulders are so tight until Josefina pats them. "Who knows? You might discover you actually like breaking the rules," she says.

I doubt it.

"And I have the perfect pattern for you to practice with," Josefina continues.

It's the second surprise of the afternoon. I have

never sewn with a pattern before! I have never sewn anything more complicated than straight stitches. That can be a little boring, but Josefina insisted that I learn the basics first. I really *must* be making progress.

I follow her to a desk in the corner of the room. She opens a drawer.

"I found this pattern in a box of donations someone brought to the library," she tells me, pulling out a paper envelope. "I knew it was just right for you."

I take the envelope from Josefina's hands and study it. The picture on the front shows two kids modeling the same vest, but in different colors.

"This is a pattern for beginners," Josefina explains. "It only has three pieces."

For beginners. Of course. I begin to frown, but Josefina goes on. "It might look very simple, but that means you can personalize it however you like. Make it your own! Be creative!"

While Josefina clears off a space for me at the cutting table, I dig through the big bin of scrap fabric that she always brings to Stitch and Share. It takes a while to find something, but I finally choose a leopard print that reminds me of something Tía Abuela would wear. I spread it out on the table. "Be creative," I tell myself.

The only problem is, I've never ignored the instructions before. Not on purpose, anyway. I'm not even sure I understand what Josefina meant when she told me to make it my own. For now, I decide to start the way she did, tracing the pattern onto the fabric with a chalk pencil. Maybe some good ideas will come to me while I work.

As I trace, I start humming Tía Abuela's song, the one Banda La Chispa will perform in the talent show—if we get the chance, that is.

Mr. Hart sighs and lets the pajama bottoms he's

working on fall to his lap. "It's been ages since I've heard that song."

Oops. I set down the chalk pencil. "Sorry," I say, "I didn't mean to hum so loudly."

Señora Garcia, one of the newest sewists in our group, shakes her head. "Don't apologize," she says as she sticks a pin into the tomato-shaped pincushion she wears around her wrist. "That song is my favorite."

"And no one could sing it like La Chispa," Mrs. Glass adds.

I swallow hard, wondering if she's right. *From now on, I'll only hum in my head*, I think, turning back to the pattern.

"You know," Josefina says, "we might be able to hear La Chispa sing it. I think we have a recording in the library. One second."

Josefina leaves the community room, and

eighty-seven seconds later (not that I'm counting) comes back with a CD from the music collection. She's also carrying a CD player, which she sets on top of the desk and plugs into the wall. She pops open the top and drops the CD inside.

Everyone stops when she presses play. Tía Abuela's voice pours through the speakers, as silky as the piece of fabric I'm working on. Mr. Hart closes his eyes. Señora Garcia sways in her chair. Then, when Tía Abuela gets to the big chorus, Mr. Hart starts singing too. Soon the whole room is singing. Even Anthony Becerra, the only other kid in Stitch and Share. Even *me*.

I wish Banda La Chispa could play exactly like this.

Maybe we can!

I have the most amazing idea.

"Señora Josefina, when Stitch and Share is over,

do you think I can borrow that CD?" I ask. "I want my friends to hear it."

If we can follow the recording exactly—the same way I'm trying to follow the lines of this sewing pattern—maybe we can get the song just right.

"Por supuesto, Catalina," Josefina agrees. "We can lend you the CD player too."

CHAPTER 4

Just Right

The last notes of the song begin to fade. When Tía Abuela's voice is barely a whisper, I look up at the rest of the band.

It's after school on Tuesday, and we're in Pablo's garage. We've agreed to meet for an hour after school each day to rehearse before Friday's auditions.

"Should we listen to it one more time?" I ask. "To make sure we have the notes exactly right?"

Soledad groans. "Catalina," she says, putting her

hand over mine before I can press the play button again. "We've already listened to it *six* times in a row. Can't we just practice the song now?"

Ruthie taps her drumsticks together. "Yeah, Cat, my mom is going to pick me up any minute. I have to get to soccer."

I turn to Pablo.

I might be La Chispa's grand-niece, but Pablo is her number one fan. He knows all of Tía Abuela's roles and has even memorized her most famous lines. Every time he sees her in person, he asks her to sign his autograph book. (She always does.) Disappointing La Chispa—getting her song wrong— is the last thing he'd want to do. I know he'll say we should listen to the recording again.

Instead Pablo folds his arms over his chest. "They never rehearse like this on *Allegro Academy*."

Soledad wrinkles her nose. "What's that?"

Pablo's eyes sparkle. Uh-oh. I know what's coming.

"You've never heard of *Allegro Academy*?" he asks, pressing his hand over his heart as if he is shocked by what she said. "It used to be my mom's favorite telenovela when she was a teenager. We've been watching it together. It's all about the students at a special high school for pop stars and—"

I clear my throat to get their attention. Pablo loves watching telenovelas—the Spanish-language TV shows, full of drama—that Tía Abuela used to star in. He could talk about his latest favorite all afternoon. We don't have time for that.

"Maybe you're right," I say. "We're ready to sing. Let's take it from the top."

Pablo huffs and steps back behind his keyboard. Ruthie sits up straighter at her drum set. I pick up my tambourine.

Once we're all settled, Soledad counts off.

We begin to play.

At first I think it's our best version yet. Listening to Tía Abuela's recording has paid off. Ruthie's beat is strong and steady. Pablo's notes sound like the ones the band played on the CD. When Soledad starts singing, her voice is fierce and fiery, exactly like Tía Abuela's. I shake my tambourine and wait to join in during the chorus.

But then, right as the first verse is about to end, Soledad changes one of the words!

I let the tambourine fall to my side. I look over my shoulder at Ruthie. She doesn't seem to have noticed. I look the other way, at Pablo. He's still playing the keyboard and bopping his head along to the rhythm. I try to ignore what I've just heard. *It's okay if we're not perfect yet*, I tell myself. *We still have a few more days to get it right.*

But it's no use. Soledad's slip-up is just too distracting.

"Wait!" I yell.

The notes all clang together, sour and awful, as the music crashes to a stop.

Pablo freezes with his fingers hovering above the keys.

Ruthie holds her drumsticks in the air.

Soledad strums one more angry chord on her guitar. "Why'd you do that?" she asks. "We sounded great!"

Maybe she doesn't realize she messed up. But that's hard to believe, especially after we listened to the song so many times.

I lower my voice. I don't want to make Soledad feel bad. "You sang the wrong word," I whisper.

"I didn't sing the wrong word!" Soledad shouts back.

At least I *tried* not to call too much attention to it.

"Are you sure, Cat?" Ruthie asks. "I didn't hear anything wrong."

Of course I'm sure. I memorized all the lyrics. I turn to Pablo again. He *must* have heard it too. His attention to detail is almost as sharp as mine. But Pablo doesn't back me up.

I sigh. "At the end of the first verse," I explain. "You made a mistake. It's supposed to be 'maleta,' and you said 'paleta.' They mean completely different things."

"Maleta" means "suitcase"—I know because I looked it up last night. And a paleta is a special kind of frozen fruit bar. I know because the strawberry ones are my favorite summer treat.

"It wasn't a mistake," Soledad says. "I did it on purpose. I thought it sounded better that way."

How could anything sound better than the *right* way?

But I take a deep breath before I say anything

else. I don't want Soledad to feel discouraged.

"Your voice sounded wonderful," I tell her finally. I really mean it too. "Especially at the beginning. But let's try practicing with the correct words. After all, we want to make sure we get a spot in the talent show, don't we?"

They all nod.

"Fine," Soledad says. "Let's try it again."

We take it from the top. This time, I count off, and when we get to the end of the verse, and Soledad sings the correct words, I look back at her and wink.

But just as I do, I notice that Pablo has changed the keyboard notes. They don't sound bad. Just . . . different.

"Wait!" I say again. This time I'm so frustrated that my tambourine slips from my fingers. It clatters to the ground.

"What now?" Soledad demands, her hand on

her hip. "I sang all the right words. Exactly like La Chispa. Exactly like you wanted me to."

It's true. She did. "You were *perfect*," I reassure Soledad. I turn around to face Pablo. "But you . . ."

"I thought it would sound more interesting if I changed the notes a little bit," Pablo explains. "If I played in harmony with Soledad."

Ruthie nods. "I loved it!"

"I got the idea from *Allegro Academy*," Pablo continues. "The characters are always trying to stand out from the crowd."

I try to stay patient, but we are running out of time. Pablo, more than anyone else, should know how important it is to get this song just right.

"But, Pablo," I say, "this isn't *Allegro Academy*." I pick up my tambourine and walk over to the CD player. "Let's listen to the real version again. Just a few more times."

CHAPTER 5

Extra Help

That night, I lie in bed with my three plush kittens lined up, shortest to tallest, beside my pillow, just the way I like them. While Coco tosses and turns on the top bunk, I think about what Tía Abuela wrote to me in her note. Banda La Chispa seems to be getting better every time we play the song. But singing all afternoon hasn't chased my worries away. In fact, it might have given me new ones.

I am pretty much sure of it: the band is going to

need a little extra help getting into the talent show. *Magical* help.

Finally Coco's breathing turns into a soft snore. Now that she is in a deep sleep, I roll out of bed and sneak to my closet. I stand on tiptoe to reach the highest shelf, where I've hidden the magical sewing kit. When my hand lands on the soft velvet pouch, a jolt shoots up my fingers, like when Coco and I shuffle across the carpet in socks and try to shock each other.

I take the sewing kit down, flip on the closet light, and then sit on the floor. There's plenty of space to work because I always keep my closet so tidy. Not like Coco's. If Mami and Papi walk by, they'll just think I'm up reading past my bedtime. They'll never guess the truth—that I'm sewing up a batch of magical disguises.

Still, I'd better hurry.

I unzip my backpack and take out the vest pattern Josefina the Librarian lent me. Then I find the big piece of purple fabric inside the box Tía Abuela sent. There should be enough to make a vest for each of the band members. And if I use the magical needle and thread, anyone who sees us wearing them will think we're *major* musicians, exactly like the ones on the recording!

Maybe Pablo was right all along. We need some-thing to help us stand out from the crowd. I spread the fabric on the floor and start tracing.

For the next two nights, after Coco has gone to bed, I do the same thing. By Friday, I have sewn four matching purple vests, one for each of us. I'm a little tired, but it was worth it.

I wait until after school on Friday, right before the auditions, to surprise the rest of the band with our new uniforms. Soledad, Ruthie, and Pablo are already lined up inside the auditorium, waiting for our turn to perform.

Ruthie picks at her nail polish. "I'm not used to drumming in front of so many people," she says, her eyes darting around the crowded room. "What if I mess up?"

Soledad pats her back. "Don't worry," she says.

"We're going to do an amazing job. We've been practicing all week."

Now is the perfect moment to show them, to unveil the little bit of magic that will guarantee that the crowd loves us—and the judges too.

"And if all that practice wasn't enough," I say, whipping a gift box from behind my back. "We have these to help us!"

I lift open the lid. Inside are four purple vests, sewn together with shimmering silver thread.

Soledad peers into the box. She pulls out one of the vests and holds it in front of her face, pinching it between her thumb and index finger like it's one of Carlos's dirty diapers.

"What's this for?" she asks.

I hold out the box to Pablo and then to Ruthie. They each take a vest. "Band uniforms, of course,"

I say. "I made them myself. Not only will we *sound* perfect, but we'll *look* perfect too. Like a real band." I don't tell them about the magic. "Quick, put them on."

Soledad frowns and tries to hand the vest back to me. "They're really nice, Cat," she says. "But I was hoping to wear something brighter. Something that will grab everyone's attention when we're onstage. Like this." She reaches into her backpack and pulls out a feathered boa. She wraps it around her neck. Pink and orange feathers flutter to the floor. "Do you like it?" she asks, twirling.

Before I can answer, Ruthie takes a red silk rose out of her pocket. "My grandma gave it to me," she says, gently cradling the flower in her palm. "I like to wear it when I have a test, or anytime I need some extra luck. I could pin it to the vest, though."

I shake my head. "But then we wouldn't match." It would ruin the whole effect.

"Pablo?" I ask. "What do you think?" Surely he'll understand how important this is to me.

"Actually, Catalina," he says, shifting from one foot to the other, "I was going to wear this tie—it's like the one the characters wear in *Allegro Academy*. I don't think I can wear it with your vest. The colors will clash."

He's right about that.

Just then the loudspeaker crackles. "Banda La Chispa, it's your turn to audition," Mr. Stevens, the music teacher, says. "Please make your way to the stage."

It's our turn, and I'm out of time! Somehow I need to get my bandmates to put on the vests. But how can I convince them without revealing the secret of the magic sewing kit?

· CHAPTER 6 ·

In the Spotlight

*P*lease wear them?" I beg. "We don't want all our practice to go to waste, all because we don't look perfectly put together."

No one moves. They just blink back at me.

"Do it for me?" I ask. "Do it for . . . La Chispa."

Pablo's shoulders slump. I knew he wouldn't be able to turn me down after I mentioned Tía Abuela. Once he changes his mind, Ruthie and Soledad do as well.

"Are you happy now?" Soledad asks.

"Very," I say. And soon the rest of the band will be too. I know it. But there isn't time to waste. Mr. Stevens's voice crackles through the speaker again.

"Banda La Chispa?"

"Vamos!" I yell. "Let's go. We can't be late!"

I race up the steps to the stage. The rest of the

band scrambles behind me as they try to put on their new vests.

We finally get into position. All the other groups waiting to audition stop what they're doing to watch. I glance down at the vest. The purple fabric gleams. The silver thread glitters.

"Look, it's Banda La Chispa!" someone calls out.

Someone else whistles.

The judges lean forward in their seats.

The disguises are working! Everyone thinks we're a real band!

Ruthie shrinks behind her drums. "Why are they staring at us like that?" she asks. "Why are they already cheering?"

I grin. "It's because they know we're going to be absolutely . . . magical!" I reply.

This must be what Tía Abuela feels like every time she stands in the spotlight, ready to perform.

This must be what she meant when she said that singing chases your worries away.

I gather the band into one last huddle.

"Let's play it exactly the way we practiced," I remind them. "The way it sounds in the recording." I turn to Ruthie. "You'll make sure to keep the beat strong and steady?"

She nods. "Y-yup," she says, before her eyes flutter back to the crowd gathering in front of the stage.

"And, Pablo," I say next, "you'll play the chords the way they were written? No special harmonies this time?"

"If you say so," he answers glumly. Then he steps out of the huddle and goes to his keyboard. I'm sure Pablo will cheer up once we earn our spot in the talent show.

Last, I come to Soledad. The crowd is chanting, "Canten! Canten!" Sing! Sing!

"And you'll say the correct words?" I ask her. "Did you remember to write them out three times last night? That always helps me memorize."

Soledad huffs. "Maybe *you'd* better sing, Catalina. That way you'll know that everything is exactly the way *you* want it." She grabs the microphone stand and moves it to my spot between Pablo and Ruthie.

I can't tell if Soledad is angry or nervous. Either way, it isn't such a bad idea. After all, I have been listening to the song, note by note, measure by measure, all week long. I know it by heart.

"You're right," I say. "I will!"

By now the cheering is so loud that we almost can't hear one another. I rattle the tambourine to get the band's attention. Then I count us off. "Uno, dos, tres, cuatro!"

Ruthie's drumming keeps us all moving at an even tempo. Pablo's keyboard notes blend perfectly with Soledad's guitar chords. The music swirls around my head as I shake my tambourine along with the beat. When I throw back my head and begin to sing, I pretend I am La Chispa. I wish she could see me now. But after this audition, I'm sure she'll get a chance to see me at the talent show next week.

We make it to the end of the song without missing a single note. I know because I've been paying attention to each and every one of them. My plan worked! We sounded just like Tía Abuela's famous recording. I'll have to tell Josefina the Librarian. Sometimes it's a good thing to follow the pattern. In sewing *and* in singing.

The crowd cheers again as we bow. I wave and

blow kisses, the same way I've seen Tía Abuela do when she finishes a spectacular performance. But then, when I turn to see if the rest of the band is enjoying the attention as much as I am, I realize they aren't there anymore. I'm all alone onstage. *They probably wanted to rush home to tell their families what a great job we all did*, I think. But even I don't quite believe it.

· CHAPTER 7 ·

Solo

*T*he hallway is already crowded when I get to Valle Grande Elementary early on Monday morning. It seems like the whole school is crammed outside the music room, where the talent show list is posted on the wall.

I nudge my way through, wishing I had a snake *disfraz* to help me get to the list faster. The other kids would step aside if they thought I was a snake.

I make a mental note to add boa constrictor to my costume wish list.

When I get to the front of the crowd, I scan the list, looking for "Banda La Chispa." I don't have to look for long. We're first on the lineup! We made it!

I can't wait to find Pablo, Soledad, and Ruthie so we can celebrate. Tía Abuela is going to hear us perform her song! And the best part is, we've already spent so much time practicing that it's sure to be a *perfect* performance. All we have to do is repeat what we did for the audition.

But my friends aren't in any of the usual places. Not swinging on the playground, not grabbing a breakfast sandwich in the cafeteria, not even reading in the library. Finally I have to head to the third-grade classroom. The bell is about to ring, and I am always on time.

To my surprise, Pablo, Soledad, and Ruthie are already there, slouching in their seats.

They must not have heard. Now I can be the one to share the amazing news.

"We made it!" I shout, breaking a major classroom rule for maybe the first time ever. But I have a very good reason. "We're in the talent show!"

I thought they would cheer. Or smile. Or even lift their eyes off the ground.

But they don't.

"Yeah," Pablo says, and shrugs, "we know."

If they know, they shouldn't look so disappointed. Maybe they're tired. I know I had a hard time falling asleep last night. My thoughts raced as I wondered if we'd made the show and worried that maybe we hadn't.

They can't still be angry over the vests, can they? Not after our performance went so well.

"If you already know, then why aren't you happy?" I ask.

Soledad looks up. She narrows her eyes behind her round glasses. For the first time, I notice the purple vest hanging over the back of her chair. *She should have left the vest at home*, I think. There's no telling what might stain it at school. A pen could leak. Chocolate milk could spill. You could slip and fall on the grass. And we want our costumes to look fresh and clean at the talent show on Friday.

But I don't mention it. I almost couldn't resist wearing my vest to school either.

"We are not performing," Soledad says.

I'm so surprised that I leap backward. "Of course we are," I argue. "You just heard me, didn't you? We got in."

Soledad shakes her head. "I know we got in, but we're quitting the band. It was fun at the beginning, when we were all trying our best and trying new things," she says. "But ever since we started copying the original—singing it over and over again, exactly the same way—it's gotten kind of . . . boring."

"Not just *kind of*," Pablo mutters.

Soledad takes the vest from the back of her

chair and holds it out to me. "Here," she says. "I don't think I was cut out to be in Banda La Chispa after all."

I take the vest, only because I'm worried that if I don't, it'll fall to the floor.

"But what about everyone cheering for us?" I ask. "They wouldn't have cheered like that if we hadn't done a great job."

Next Ruthie holds out her vest. "It was awful," she confesses, her voice shaky. "I was so worried I was going to mess up that my stomach hurt all day. I'm leaving the band too."

I didn't know she felt that way. I can't stand messing up either—that's why I wanted to practice so much.

"Well," I say, walking toward Pablo's desk, "I guess it's just you and me. But don't worry. Tía Abuela is going to love us, even if we're not playing

with the whole band anymore."

Pablo sighs. He unzips his book bag and takes out his vest, folded into a neat purple square.

"I'm not performing either," he says softly, setting the vest on the corner of my desk.

"But why?" I ask, taking another step toward him. "Don't you want to perform for La Chispa? Isn't this your dream?"

Pablo keeps staring down at the floor without saying anything. Then the tips of his ears begin to turn pink. Next the color spreads to his cheeks. These are not good signs.

"It was my dream until you took over," Pablo says, turning to me. "I had some good ideas, but you wouldn't even listen to any of them. You were so focused on making everything perfect that you didn't let us make it our own. La Chispa would never have done that."

That's when the bell rings. Suddenly I am a solo act.

CHAPTER 8

INCOGNITO

I walk home by myself that afternoon. I should be walking to Pablo's house. The band agreed that if we made it into the talent show, we'd keep meeting in his garage to practice. But now there's no band. There's only me.

Even though it isn't very cold outside, I take my favorite gray sweatshirt out of my backpack. I always carry it with me, but it wasn't always my favorite. Especially after Tía Abuela sewed kitten ears onto the hood. (No one *ever* listens when I tell them I'm getting too old for all the kitten stuff.)

But then I realized that Tía Abuela had sewn the ears on with magic. That means the sweatshirt is more than a sweatshirt. It's also a disfraz. Which makes it just what I need. Right now I feel like hiding, and going incognito is the next-best thing.

I push my arms through the sweatshirt sleeves and pull the zipper up to my neck.

Next I look around to make sure no one is watching. I pull the hood over my head, and a shiver runs up my spine. When I look down at my shadow on the sidewalk, I don't see the shadow of a girl anymore. I see the shadow of a cat.

As I dart behind cars and hedges and garbage cans, I wonder how I'm going to pull off the talent show performance on my own. My bandmates— *former* bandmates, that is—are being so unfair.

They wanted to make it into the talent show, didn't they? Thanks to me, we did.

When I'm almost back to my house, I hear the rumble of skateboard wheels rolling over the street.

Coco.

It's lucky I'm incognito. I'm not ready to tell my family what happened with the band. They'll find out soon enough when I'm the only one onstage at the talent show on Friday.

I drop my backpack and crouch behind the neighbor's rosebush to watch.

Coco is working on her kick flip. I know because I've seen her practice the trick on the street in front of our house every weekend for the past month. Over and over and over.

She must be getting ready for Tía Abuela's visit too. This surprises me because Coco doesn't always appreciate good preparation. You should see her

rushing to pack up her school supplies at the very last minute every morning.

But as I watch, I realize that Coco isn't doing the same trick over and over. She's doing *almost* the same trick, but a little different each time. Once, she lands with her legs crossed, one over the other. The next time, she lands on one foot.

Not Coco too! "Why don't you just do it the *right* way?" I shout as she prepares to do the trick again. Only, the words don't come out in my voice. They come out like the yowl of an angry cat.

Whoops. I forgot all about the disfraz. I try to scamper away before Coco sees me. But it's too late. She hops off her skateboard.

"Hey," she says, turning around. "You ruined my trick."

I want to tell her that *she* ruined it herself with all those changes. But I don't dare move a whisker.

Coco squints at me. "You look sorta familiar," she says. "You must be that cat Mami is always complaining about. The one who hangs around our house like she lives there."

I *do* live there. But Coco doesn't know that. I skitter backward and dive behind the roses.

I'm crawling away when a thorn pricks my wrist.

"Ouch!" I yelp.

It comes out in my real voice. Oh no! I touch the top of my head and realize I'm not wearing the hood anymore. It must have snagged on one of the thorns. I am no longer incognito.

"Is that . . . Cat?"

Slowly I stand. Coco watches with her eyes wide, her mouth hanging open. "Have you been hiding in the bushes the whole time?"

"I . . . um . . . ," I sputter, trying to think of an explanation. "Yes! I was watching you skate, but I didn't want to disturb you." I brush some rose petals off my leggings.

Coco comes closer, like she doesn't believe me. She peers into the bush. "There was a cat just now—right here, right where you're standing," she says. "Did you see her?"

I look behind me, pretending to search for the mystery cat that I know isn't there anymore.

"Maaaybe," I answer, "but she must have run away." I change the subject. "What are you working on? I thought you already perfected your kick flip."

Coco tightens the strap of her helmet under her chin. "I did," she says. "But now I want to put my own personal stamp on it. I've always wanted to have a trick named after me. Watch this."

Coco jumps back onto her skateboard, and I sit on the curb to watch. She pushes off. Once she's rolling, she steps down hard on the back of the board to pop it into the air. Then she flicks the board with her front foot so it spirals under her feet. When she comes back

down, she lands on the back two wheels, the skateboard's nose pointing in the air.

It was so exciting, I don't even mind that she didn't do the trick the right way. "Bravo!" I say, and clap.

Coco unfastens her helmet. "What did you think of that one?" she asks. "Tell me the truth."

I tap my finger against my lips. "Hmmm . . . I think you should call it the Coco-kick."

CHAPTER 9

Sew Busy

The longer I watch Coco trying out new ways to land her skateboard trick, the more I understand why Pablo, Soledad, and Ruthie were so frustrated with me. They wanted to sing Tía Abuela's song, but they didn't want to sing it just like Tía Abuela. They wanted to make it their own. They wanted the song to fit their styles the same way Josefina the Librarian wanted the dress she was sewing to fit her style.

As soon as Coco and I get home, I race upstairs to

our bedroom. I open my sketchbook to a fresh page and take my colored pencils out of their drawer. It's a good thing I always keep them sharpened. I get to work, and when I'm finished, there's barely enough time to make it to Stitch and Share.

"I was getting worried," Josefina the Librarian says as I burst through the doors. "You're usually here so early."

Early to Josefina is right on time for me.

I look around the room as I catch my breath. For once, some of the other sewists have arrived before me. That's a good thing. At Stitch and Share, there's always someone to help if you need it. And I need plenty.

Josefina notices the bundles of fabric I'm carrying under one arm and the drawings I'm holding in the other.

She claps.

"Oh good!" she says. "It looks like you've come up with an idea for the vest you started last week. I knew you'd think of a way to make it your own."

I drop my supplies onto the cutting table that's still set up in the center of the room. "I haven't thought of *one* idea," I tell her. "I thought of *three*."

I wave the other sewists over. "My friends and I are supposed to perform in the school talent show on Friday," I explain. "At first I thought we should all match, but that didn't work very well. Now I want to try something *different*."

I spread out my drawings. Three different vests to match three different personalities. "But I'm going to need some help," I finish.

Josefina the Librarian picks up one of the sketches. "You didn't just make the pattern your own," she says. "You made your own patterns!"

I hold my breath, hoping Josefina doesn't mind

that I ignored the instructions completely. I'm nervous that she'll say I need more practice before I can sew these new vests.

Instead she says, "Excelente, Catalina! These

are even better than the original. I'll help you. Does anyone else have time to set aside their projects to work on Catalina's costumes?"

Señora Garcia takes the drawing I made of Soledad's vest. She squints at it. "Sequins can be very tricky to sew with," she says. "Luckily, I just sewed a mermaid costume for my neighbor that was covered in sequins. I can show you all the tricks I learned."

Mr. Hart picks up the sketch of Ruthie's vest. "This one has the same shape as a fishing vest I made not too long ago," he says. "I can help you make a pattern piece." He gets up off his folding chair and makes his way to the desk in the corner to find some drawing paper.

"And I have some buttons in my collection that will match perfectly," Ms. Yoo says. "I'll show you how to stitch them on so they never come loose."

For the rest of Stitch and Share, I flutter from chair to chair, almost as if I am still wearing my butterfly wings. When Anthony and Mrs. Glass arrive, they join other sewists in helping me bring my costume designs to life—*without* any magic.

By the time the session is over, the new vests are ready and even better than I imagined. I pack them up with the rest of my sewing supplies, careful not to let them wrinkle.

"Don't forget this one," Josefina the Librarian says. She holds up a leopard-print vest. It's the one I started last week at Stitch and Share, when I didn't know how to make a pattern my own. I had forgotten all about it.

"I noticed you hadn't designed a costume for yourself, so I thought I'd finish this one for you," she says. I was so busy—more like *sew* busy—that I didn't even notice her working on it.

"And I added something special, just for you," Josefina continues.

"Pockets?" I ask. Pockets would be very useful. I could keep a spare needle and thread inside, just in case of sewing emergencies.

"No," Josefina says, turning the vest around to reveal . . . a tail. "Isn't it *purr*-fect?"

I sigh. More kittens. Of course.

Still, I take the vest and fold it with the others. "Gracias!" I shout as I wave goodbye.

CHAPTER 10

EVEN BETTER

It's Friday, and Banda La Chispa is still on the talent show lineup. I just hope there's still a band.

The talent show is set to begin right after lunch. I watch from backstage with the rest of the performers as kids begin to fill the auditorium, kindergartners in the first rows and sixth graders near the back. Behind them, teachers set out chairs for parents and other relatives. Soon Tía Abuela will be sitting in one of them. She said she'd be coming straight from the airport. I hope she won't be too disappointed when she doesn't see me onstage.

Because if my plan works out, I might not be singing.

Finally the third graders file into the auditorium. Mr. Stevens is so busy backstage that he doesn't notice me step out from behind the curtain to find Pablo, Soledad, and Ruthie in the audience. He doesn't notice the box I'm carrying either.

"Shouldn't you be getting ready to sing?" Pablo asks when I make my way to his seat. He gives his watch a nervous glance. "There's only a few more minutes before the show starts. Aren't you worried you'll be late?"

I'm worried *he'll* be late. Pablo and the rest of the band. "That's why I'm here," I say. "I want the band—all of you—to sing the song. I'm sorry I didn't listen to your ideas before. I was afraid that if we changed the song, we'd ruin it. But now I under-stand that you were trying to make it even better."

Soledad points to the box tucked under my arm. "What's that?" She wrinkles her nose. "Not the vests again?"

"Not exactly," I say, taking off the lid. "I changed the pattern. The vests don't match anymore. But this time, they might actually fit you."

The first vest goes to Ruthie. It's made out of the zebra-print fabric that Tía Abuela sent from Colombia. "I know you love animal accessories," I explain. "And I thought your grandma's red rose would look great with the black-and-white fabric."

Ruthie hugs the vest to her chest. "I love it!" she exclaims.

The next one is for Soledad. It's covered in pink and orange sequins that shimmer in the light. "You told me you wanted to stand out onstage," I say.

"Well, no one will be able to miss you in this. It even goes with your feather boa."

Soledad grabs the vest before I've even finished explaining. "It's perfect!" she says, holding it up in front of her face. The auditorium lights bounce off the sequins and dance in her glasses.

I catch Pablo trying to sneak a peek at the box out of the corner of his eye.

Carefully I remove his vest. "And I made this one especially for you, Pablo," I say.

When he sees the vest, his eyes widen. It's red with blue trim.

"This looks exactly like the uniform on—"

"*Allegro Academy!*" I finish the sentence for him. "I know! Josefina the Librarian searched for pictures online so I could get the details just right." I frown. "I didn't have enough time to make the tie, though."

Pablo smiles. He reaches into his pocket and

pulls out a striped tie. "I always come prepared," he replies.

There's one more thing to say, and I'd better hurry because the show is about to start. The principal is already at the front of the stage, trying to settle everyone down.

"You don't have to wear the vests," I whisper. "But I wanted you to know that I really *was* listening. Your ideas will make Tía Abuela's song better than ever. You should perform it instead of me."

My eyes begin to sting. I blink to stop myself from crying. I don't want to miss my chance in the spotlight—my chance to impress Tía Abuela—but I know she'll be proud of my progress. And not just in sewing.

"Vamos!" Soledad shouts. I watch her, Pablo, and Ruthie jump from their seats and start making their way backstage. Just as I'm about to slump down into Pablo's empty spot, Soledad pauses and looks over her shoulder.

"Aren't you coming?" she asks. "The show's going to start any second. And you know what Pablo says. 'Late is late.'"

"Really?" I almost can't believe it. They were so upset with me after the audition.

Pablo stops too. "Of course," he says. "If you hadn't made us practice so much, we wouldn't sound as good as we do."

"But what will you wear?" Ruthie asks. "We all have these great new costumes, and you don't have anything."

Luckily, there's one more vest in the box. "Don't worry," I say, putting on the leopard-print vest that Josefina the Librarian made me. I brought it just in case. "I have something *purr-fect*."

CHAPTER 11

A Perfect Performance

A few of us peek out from behind the curtains as Aaron Chu finishes his magic act with a swish of his cape. This time, a bouquet of daisies pops up out of his hat. We cheer along with the audience.

When Aaron finishes his bows, Esme and Jazmín walk onstage together. They have matching ribbons in their braids. As they dance, their swirling blue skirts look like flowers opening and closing. The sound of their stamping boots echoes through the auditorium.

They don't miss a step.

We clap again as their song ends. "It's almost time," I whisper to myself.

"Next up," Mr. Stevens announces, "is Banda La Chispa."

Pablo, Soledad, Ruthie, and I take the stage. As Mr. Stevens helps Pablo set up his keyboard, I peer out into the audience. Mami and Papi smile back at me. Baby Carlos laughs on Mami's lap. But the chair next to Papi's is empty. Tía Abuela hasn't arrived yet. After so much work, I hope she doesn't miss our performance!

I help Soledad adjust her microphone. But before we're finished, she says, "Wait. What if we *all* sing?"

The rest of the band looks at me. "Well . . ." I hesitate.

We've never practiced singing the whole song together. And it's definitely not the way Tía Abuela performed it. I'm not sure this is the right time to change things up. But then, I remind myself, sometimes experimenting with new ideas can be fun.

"Let's do it!" I say.

Quickly we move the microphone stand to the middle of the stage, where it will pick up all of our voices.

Finally it's time to sing.

My heart thumps as Soledad begins counting off.

"Uno, dos—"

Just then I hear a *click-clack, click-clack* on the auditorium floor. I know who it is without even looking.

Tía Abuela. She is wearing her favorite high-heeled boots and her cat-eye sunglasses with rhinestones in the corners. She made it!

"Perdón!" she says as she squeezes her way

across the row to the empty seat next to Papi. "I'm sorry I'm late."

Tía Abuela isn't late, though. She is right on time.

I wave, and she waves back. She lowers her sunglasses and gives the band a wink.

That's our signal. "Vamos!" I yell.

Ruthie's drumbeat is faster than ever, and I laugh, trying to match the rhythm with my tambourine.

Pablo tries out new harmonies on the keyboard, and Soledad changes a few more words. Sometimes we aren't singing the same lyrics, but we're all singing from the heart.

I don't know if Tía Abuela will like it, but I know we're having fun.

The whole audience whistles and claps along— and we didn't even need magical disguises.

When Soledad strums her last chord, Tía Abuela is the first to leap to her feet.

"Bravo!" she cries. The rest of the audience jumps up and joins her in cheering. Banda La Chispa bows—together this time. Soledad and Pablo blow kisses at the audience.

At the end of the show, after helping to pack up the instruments, I try to find Tía Abuela. As usual, a crowd of fans has swarmed her. As usual, Pablo is at the center of it, asking for yet *another* autograph.

When she finishes sign- ing, Tía Abuela wraps her arms around me and squeezes tight.

"That was unlike any- thing I have ever heard before," she tells me.

In other words, it was *perfect*.

Turn the page for a
sneak peek at Catalina's
next magical adventure!

SKATEBOARD SLUMP

I sharpen my colored pencils into perfect points and arrange them in rainbow order, just like I do every Saturday morning. That way, they are always ready when I need them.

I'm working at the kitchen table so that my baby brother, Carlos, who is rolling toy trucks on the floor with Papi, doesn't disturb me. You can't be too careful with Carlos around. I've found his tiny teeth marks on my school supplies before!

Right as I am about to place parakeet green next to lemon yellow, my big sister stomps past and bumps into my shoulder. She knocks my hand into the box of colored pencils and sends them tumbling to the floor.

"Coco!" I yell. She has never appreciated the importance of a good organization system. But that doesn't mean she can ruin mine. "Be careful!"

"Sorry, Cat," Coco says. She is carrying her skateboard and sets it down to help me pick up the pencils. At first, I try to keep them all in rainbow order. But then Carlos comes crawling toward us, drool dribbling off his bottom lip. I scramble to collect the rest of them as quickly as I can.

"What's the rush, Coco?" Papi asks as he scoops Carlos back onto his lap. Mami won't be back from her shift at the nursing home until dinnertime.

Coco puts the candy-apple-red pencil next to the midnight-blue one, nowhere near where it belongs.

"Can I go out skateboarding?" she asks.

She is already wearing her helmet and pads, and her old flannel shirt is balled up under her arm. It's going to be a wrinkled mess when she puts it on.

"Have you made your bed?" Papi asks.

"Of course!" Coco replies.

"Ha!" I bark.

Coco's idea of making the bed is piling her pajamas, sheets, and blanket on top of it in a lumpy heap. I should know. I have to share a room with her.

But Papi seems convinced. "Have fun," he says. "Be careful."

I take the red pencil out of the box and put it back where it's supposed to be—next to tangerine orange. "Wait up," I say. "Give me a minute to put the rest of these pencils away, and I'll come too."

Coco has been helping me learn to skateboard. Since all my chores are finished—including some that Mami and Papi didn't even think of—I can go with her to learn some new tricks.

"No!" Coco says.

"No?" I repeat. Coco doesn't always let me borrow her board, but she's never said I couldn't come with her to skate.

"I really need to concentrate this time," she says. "I need to be alone."

I turn to Papi. "Por favor. Pleeeeeeeease," I say, begging in two languages.

It doesn't work.

"Sorry, Kitty-Cat," Papi says. "Sounds like Coco needs her space."

Being called "Kitty-Cat" is pretty annoying. I've asked my parents about a zillion times to start using my real name, "Catalina." But even more annoying is not getting to go out with Coco. I grab the pencil box and storm upstairs to our room.

Not that I plan to stay there.

As soon as I hear Coco's skateboard rattle down the sidewalk, I go to my closet. I pick out my favorite sweatshirt. It's gray with kitten ears sewn onto the hood. My tía abuela—her name is "Catalina Castañeda" too—sewed it for me. Normally, I wouldn't wear it. Like I keep telling my Mami and Papi, I'm getting too old for all the kitten stuff. But today the sweatshirt is exactly what I need.

I creep back down the stairs, tiptoe down the hall, and sneak out the side door.

Then, flattening myself against the house so that no one can see, I put on the sweatshirt. I zip it up to my chin. I pull the hood over my head. A shiver runs up my spine. I check my reflection in one of the windows. A gray cat blinks back at me. I am incognito.

Tía Abuela didn't make the sweatshirt with

a regular needle and thread. She used a special sewing kit with the power to create magical disguises. Better yet, she passed the magic on to me!

I trot down the street to find Coco. She might have said I couldn't watch her skateboard, but she didn't say anything about a *cat* watching.

I find Coco at the end of the block. She must really not want anyone to see her.

I can understand why. She's wearing her flannel, but it's way too short, and her elbow pokes out of a hole in the sleeve. I shudder. I wouldn't want to be seen in that thing either.

Then again, Coco doesn't care very much about what anyone else thinks of her clothes. Something else must be bothering her. I step closer and stop to watch under the shade of a blue mailbox.

Coco tightens her helmet. She wipes her palms against her shorts and takes off.

I recognize this move. It's her signature trick, the Coco-kick. She steps down onto the back of the board and launches it into the air. Next she's supposed to flick the board with her toe so it spins underneath her. Instead, she kicks it off to the side and lands on her knees.

Ouch.

She tries an easier trick, one she has landed millions of times. But she just keeps crashing.

"What's going on?" I ask. Only, I'm still incognito and it comes out like a curious purr. Coco lifts her head off the sidewalk where she's still sprawled.

"I was hoping nobody saw that," she said. "But you won't tell, will you?" She sits up and scoots closer to me. "You seem familiar. Have I seen you before?"

I skitter backward.

Coco shakes her head and unbuckles her

helmet. "I need to land the Coco-kick for the Skate Spectacular," she says. "It has to be perfect. But I can't seem to get anything right. I might as well go home."

Home? Uh-oh.